PARENTS' MAGAZINE PRESS, INC.
52 Vanderbilt Ave., New York 17, N. Y.

NINE FINE GIFTS

by *Evelyn White Minshull & Naiad Einsel*

I had a birthday
not long ago.
I got a lot of gifts,
but none to show.
For I lost them.
All of them.
Nine of them.
There were
three flower seeds
from the lady next door,
and two sugar cubes
(she had no more),
a cocoon from a bush,
red silk from a kite,
and a squirrel who
crawled into my room
that night.

Aren't those fine?
But that's eight,
not nine.
There was another,
from my mother.
And it was best.
Better and finer
than all the rest.
She made a jacket
for you know who,
with big, big pockets.
(Deep ones, too.)

So that was my birthday—
part of it, anyway.

I put eight of the gifts
into one of the pockets
of my new jacket.
The three flower seeds
from the lady next door,
and two sugar cubes
(since there were no more),
the cocoon from a bush,
red silk from a kite,
and the squirrel who
crawled into my room
that night.
(He wasn't very big, really.
And my pockets
were *quite* big.
They had to be,
to hold
all of those things!)

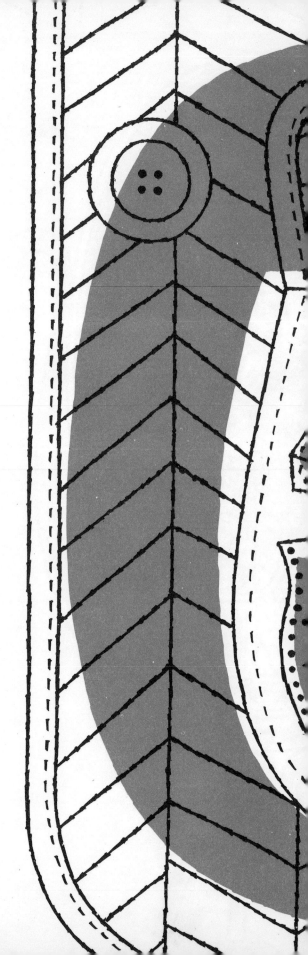

Well, I walked down the path, for it wasn't late,
down the path to the garden gate.
And that was where I lost the flower seeds.
I didn't take them out or shake them out.
They didn't fall out but they were all out.

Because the squirrel, you see, deep down in my jacket,
was chewing and chewing without any racket.
Quiet as quiet.
He chewed a little hole. Not big, but big enough.
And oh-oh! What do you know!
The seeds, my lovely flower seeds were gone!

Of course, I still had
the two sugar cubes,
the cocoon from a bush,
red silk from a kite,
and the squirrel (the naughty thing)
from my room that night.
And the jacket, of course.

But not for long!
For the sugar cubes fell out.
Right on the hill,
near the very top,
they both fell out
with a soft *plop plop*.
The hole in my pocket
was a little bigger, you see.
And that naughty little squirrel
was still quite busy!
Gnawing and chewing
without a sound,
losing my gifts,
so they couldn't be found.
And oh-oh!
What do you know!
The sugar cubes were gone!

Of course, I still had
the cocoon from a bush,
red silk from a kite,
and the squirrel (nasty thing)
from my room that night.
And the jacket.

Well, the woods were close by,
so I took a look,
to see if there were fish
in the clear, cool brook;
to see if the beavers
were cutting trees;
to see if the flowers
liked the breeze.
And the hole in my pocket
got bigger and bigger.
The squirrel chewed and chewed.
Then oh-oh, what do you know!
The cocoon fell out!

What a birthday!
Well, it really wasn't *too* bad,
for I still had
the red silk from a kite
and the squirrel
(the bad little fellow)
who came to my room
that night.
And the jacket.

It was getting late,
and I was tired.
But the squirrel wasn't.
No sir!
Snip-snip and
chew-chew-chew!
A little bit here
and that will do!
And oh-oh!
What do you know!
My red silk was gone, too!

But I still had the squirrel (the bad boy)
who crawled into my room that night.

Then *he* jumped out, too!

All of a sudden,
my pocket was empty.
I put in my hand.
There was nothing there!

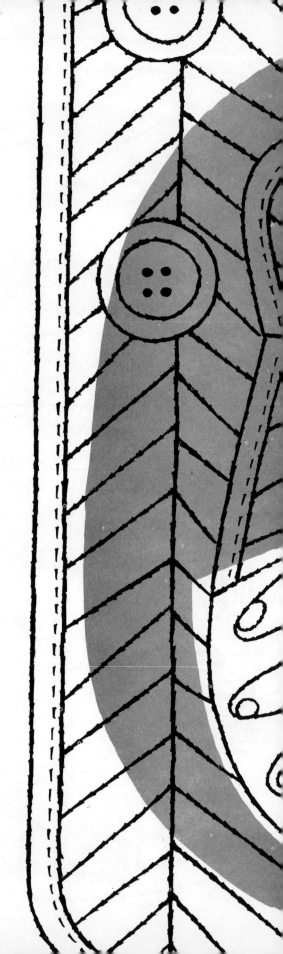

Oh, dear!
No three flower seeds
from the lady next door.
No two sugar cubes,
not any more!
No cocoon from a bush,
red silk from a kite,
or squirrel who crawled
into my room that night!
Just a jacket, with a big bite
out of the pocket!

What a birthday!

So I went home. I put my jacket on my bed
and went to wash my face and head.
And when I came back,
oh-oh! What do you know! Even the jacket was gone!

Whew!

Well, a few days later,
the jacket was back,
all cleaned and tended,
the pocket well-mended.
But I never got the other
things back,
no sir!
Not the three flower seeds
from the lady next door,
the two sugar cubes,
not any more,
the cocoon from the bush,
silk from a kite,
or the squirrel
(I wished I'd never seen him)
who crawled into my room
that night.

I never got any of these things back. Not exactly.
But maybe, in a way, I did. For, one day in the woods,
from a hollow tree, a little squirrel chattered
down at me. He shook his tail in a friendly way,
and bobbed his head as if to say, "Remember me?"
So, maybe I *did* find my squirrel, after all.

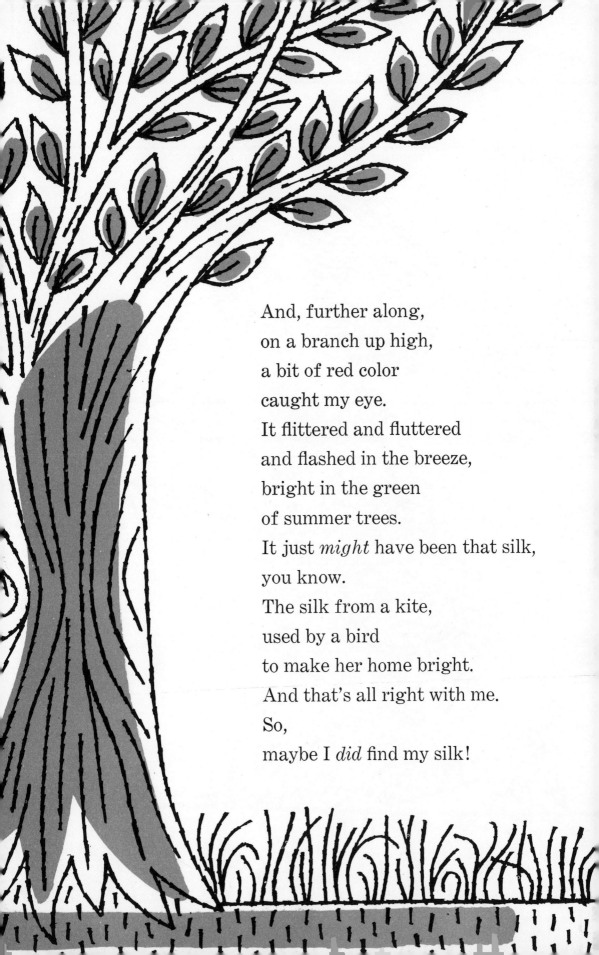

And, further along,
on a branch up high,
a bit of red color
caught my eye.
It flittered and fluttered
and flashed in the breeze,
bright in the green
of summer trees.
It just *might* have been that silk,
you know.
The silk from a kite,
used by a bird
to make her home bright.
And that's all right with me.
So,
maybe I *did* find my silk!

Then, once, as I bent above a brook,
to try to catch a fish on a bent-pin hook,

a butterfly fluttered by.

Maybe it was from the cocoon I had found on the bush.

Of course, I didn't find the sugar cubes.
But, a little pony I sometimes see
came up one day, quite close to me.
He sniffed at my pocket as if to say,
"Well, you had sugar cubes in there *one* day!"
So, maybe they weren't really lost, after all.

But, last of all, and this is best,
better and finer than all the rest—
right down the path, by the garden gate,
something happened that's really great.
First, three shoots, the greenest green,
pushed their way up to be seen.
And then the leaves popped out and grew,
drank up the rain and morning dew.
And flowers came!
They bloom and bloom.
I watch them every day. And *say!*
Maybe I did find my flower seeds, after all!

That's why, next year when I have a birthday,
this is what I hope I get—
Three flower seeds from the lady next door,
two sugar cubes (and maybe more),
a cocoon from a bush, red silk from a kite,
and a squirrel to come to my room that night.

And a jacket, of course. A jacket with pockets big and deep, but not too strong.

Not too strong for a little squirrel to chew through.